This book belongs to

....

Written by Tim Bugbird
Illustrated by Lara Ede
Designed by Annie Simpson

Copyright © 2011

make believe ideas ltd

27 Castle Street, Berkhamsted, Hertfordshire, HP4 2DW, UK.
565, Royal Parkway, Nashville, TN 37214, USA.

www.makebelieveideas.com

Camilla
the Cupcake Fairy

Tim Bugbird · Lara Ede

make
believe
ideas

On **Camilla's** fifth birthday,

the Pink Fairy Post

sent to Camilla what she

dreamed of most.

Not a **hat,** or a **doll,** or a **plant** in a pot,

or anything else she'd already got.

fairy garden

She **tore** off the paper and **giggled** with glee.

"A **wand!**" cried Camilla.

"And meant just for **me!**"

It was so very shiny and sparkly and new.
Her very first wand! But **what** would it **do**?

If she **waved** it carefully
and closed her eyes **tight**,

could she wish for a **party** with dancing all night?

Or if she sat nicely,
not making a noise,
would it make her bed neatly
and put away toys?

Or would it put on a **show** with a *dancing* dog,

The answer was no!

But what it would make,

Camilla was told, was

frosting for cake!

So she found a plain cupcake,

which she placed by her feet,

her wand at the ready,

to make a pink treat!

And holding the wand, Camilla stood straight.

She took a deep breath but just could not wait . . .

She waved it so fast,

the wand would not stop

whirling and twirling

and flashing on top!

It jumped and it jerked,

with a rattle and a shake,

it jiggled and it juddered

'til she thought

it would break!

Then, with a BANG, bright stars filled the air.

She looked for sweet frosting, but the cupcake was bare!

And there on the top, not making a sound, was a tiny white mouse, with eyes bright and round!

So she started again, this time taking care to wave the wand gently. But look what was there!

Covering the cake where the frosting should be . . .

mashed potato was all she could see!

So she tried one more **wave**, not too **fast** or too **slow**.

Now topping the cake there was nothing but . . . **snow!**

Well, snowballs and snowmen
she didn't much mind,
but this **fancy frosting**
was just the
wrong kind!

"Oh dear," thought Camilla.
"This just isn't right.
My wand is not working,
I'll be here all night!"

But then, when it seemed she was down on her luck,

Ms. Sprinkles drove by in her pink fairy truck.

Camilla asked nicely, "What should I do?"

Her teacher said kindly, "I'll give you a clue!"

"Working alone is never much fun,
but with help from your friends, the job is soon done!"

So she called her **friends** on her pink *fairy* phone.

Molly and Maya were glad to be home.

Said Molly to Maya,
"Our friend's in a state!
Let's **fly** to Camilla,
this problem
won't wait!"

They held the **wand** steady with eyes closed tight. As they worked hard together, it shone a **bright** light.

Then crossing their fingers in a shower of gold **twinkles**, they all **wished** together for frosting and **sprinkles!**

All of a sudden, the fairy friends found the tastiest treat, just there on the ground.

With sparkling sprinkles and frosting so sweet,

the best-ever cupcake was right at their feet!

So the wand could work wonders, but nothing compared to the gift of true friendship the three fairies shared!